THE CHROMA'S CLUTCHES

THE CHROMA'S CLUTCHES

By Tracey West

Random House 🏠 New York

Manufactured under license granted to AMEET Sp. z o.o. by the LEGO Group.

AMEET Sp. z o.o.
Nowe Sady 6, 94-102 Łódź—Poland
ameet@ameet.eu
www.ameet.eu

www.LEGO.com

Published in the United States by Random House Children's Books, a division of Penguin Random House LLC, 1745 Broadway, New York, NY 10019, and in Canada by Penguin Random House Canada Limited, Toronto. Random House and the colophon are registered trademarks of Penguin Random House LLC.

rhcbooks.com

ISBN 978-0-593-56569-8 (trade) — ISBN 978-0-593-56570-4 (lib. bdg.)
ISBN 978-0-593-56571-1 (ebook)

Printed in the United States of America
10 9 8 7 6 5 4 3 2 1

First Edition 2022

CONTENTS

Prologue

"I hope we get to practice our ninja skills on this call," Kai said. The Fire Ninja's eyes gleamed with anticipation.

Kai and the rest of the ninja team were walking in Ninjago City with Master Wu. The streets were crowded with people going to work and school.

"The Ninjago Museum of History just asked us to investigate some missing jewelry pieces," his sister, Nya, remarked. "It sounds pretty routine."

"Sis, nothing's *ever* routine when we go to the museum," Kai pointed out.

Jay nodded. "Yeah, we battled Aspheera and her Pyro Vipers here."

"And don't forget that we found the secret lab of the evil Time Twins in the museum, too," added Cole.

Zane made some quick calculations with his Nindroid brain. "The odds are good that we will encounter some danger here."

"And if we do, we'll be ready for it . . . like we always are," said Lloyd, the leader of the ninja.

Master Wu sighed. "Do not go looking for trouble, ninja. There is always plenty of trouble looking for *us*," he said.

They walked past the columns at the museum entrance and stepped inside. The interior of the museum always seemed to be changing. Today the main hall held a gallery of nature-inspired art. A huge oil painting showed a forest of green pine trees, and another showed a flowing waterfall. Wooden pedestals held sculptures of creatures including butterflies, a deer, and a rabbit.

"Nothing dangerous so far," Cole remarked. "Just some very nice art."

"Yeah, look at that bird statue over there," Jay said, pointing to a sculpture of a bird with black, white, and blue feathers. "It's so lifelike!"

Squawk!

The bird flew off the pedestal, right past Master Wu's face, and soared down a hallway.

"Ah!" Master Wu cried, and he jumped backward.

"Master Wu, it's just a bird," Kai said.

Master Wu nodded. "I know. I was afraid when I thought I saw a piece of art spring to life. It brought back a rather frightening memory."

Nya's eyes widened. "Oh, I hope this is another one of your stories about the journey you took with your brother, Garmadon, when you were younger."

"Indeed it is," Master Wu confirmed. "But now is not the time to tell it."

"On the contrary, I believe now *is* a good time," Zane remarked. "That bird appears to be a magpie, which is an obvious clue to our mystery. You can tell us while we search the museum for the bird."

Kai sighed. "If the jewel thief turns out to be a bird, then this is going to be a big letdown."

"Anytime Zane wants us to follow a bird, we should do it," Lloyd said. "Remember when he used to follow that falcon? It always led us to major discoveries."

Master Wu agreed. "That is true," he said. "And I shall tell you my tale while we search. But when I have finished, you may never look at a painting the same way again."

Chapter 1
The Misty Mountain

The sons of the First Spinjitzu Master slowly made their way up a tall mountain. A light mist surrounded them, almost as though they were walking through clouds. At their feet, the path looked like it had been created by animals, not humans. Through the mist they could see colorful flowers growing along the trail, and birds flittering from branch to branch, singing pretty songs.

It was a beautiful scene, almost magical, but one of the ninja was not in a good mood.

"Follow the North Star," Wu grumbled, using his staff as he climbed. "Maybe if we had asked for directions, we would have found our way to the Northern Ocean without running into this mountain."

"Aw, come on, Wu," Garmadon said, keeping pace a few steps ahead of his brother. "Father had us climbing up and down mountains all the time back home. We'll be on the other side in no time."

"It's not the climb that's bothering me," his brother replied. "There's something that's bugging me about this place."

Garmadon stopped and looked around. "Are you kidding? It's beautiful here."

"That's the point," Wu said. "It's *too* perfect. I'm suspicious. I bet there's a monster lurking behind one of these trees, waiting to attack us."

Garmadon rolled his eyes. "Relax, brother! Just because we've encountered creepy monsters on every leg of this trip doesn't mean we're going to meet one on this mountain," he said. "In fact, I'll bet that the Northern Ocean is just on the other side! We'll find that tea plant Father wants, make some tea, and see if it cures whatever imaginary problem Father thinks I have. And then this whole pointless adventure will be over."

Is it really pointless? Wu wondered, but he didn't dare ask the question out loud. The whole adventure had been set into motion because their father was worried about the increasing darkness he saw growing in Garmadon. Darkness caused by the bite of a serpent. He said the tea would cure Garmadon, and if that was true, well, that didn't feel pointless to Wu.

Wu had seen signs of his brother giving into the darkness on this journey to find the tea plant, and it worried him. Most of the time, he was the brother Wu knew—fearless, curious, impatient, and outgoing. But lately Garmadon had sometimes seemed more selfish, looking out for only himself, which was not the way of the ninja. And most of all, it was not anything like the way Garmadon had ever behaved before. Wu would be relieved when they finally found the tea.

"I hope you're right about this mountain," Wu said. "But what's that up ahead? It looks like we're walking right into the clouds."

Pale white clouds hung in the air just ahead of them. Wu stopped. "What should we do?"

"Keep going. What else? It's just fog," Garmadon replied, and he marched into the mist.

Wu sighed and followed him. He still had a bad feeling, but he wasn't about to let Garmadon face things alone. He couldn't see his brother until he bumped into him.

"How are we supposed to get anywhere when we can't see anything?" Wu complained.

"This fog won't last forever," Garmadon said. "Just keep moving, and—"

Follow me! Follow me!

There was a rustling in the bushes, and then something quickly ran across the path in front of them and disappeared into the mist.

Wu froze. "What was that?"

Garmadon shrugged. "You mean that rabbit?"

"If it was a rabbit, then it's a talking rabbit," Wu said. "It asked us to follow it. Didn't you hear it?"

Garmadon laughed. "Right. Because there are so many talking rabbits in Ninjago. You're just spooked, Wu. And even if you're right, we've seen stranger things than talking rabbits. Come on. Keep going."

"Yeah, and those stranger things were pretty dangerous," Wu muttered as Garmadon forged ahead. So far on their journey to find the tea they'd encountered a cat ninja, living puppets with stolen souls, giant scorpions, undead ghouls . . . and more.

The mist became a little thinner. The path under their feet became wider and more defined. Suddenly, both boys heard more rustling nearby.

"Probably that rabbit again," Garmadon guessed out loud.

Then a small creature hopped out of the bushes, stopped, and stared at them. It didn't look like a rabbit or any other woodland creature. This animal had a furry brown body and floppy dog ears, but it walked on two legs. It also had the long arms and tail of a monkey.

"Follow me!" the creature cried, and then it ran ahead and disappeared into the fog.

"You had to have heard *that*," Wu said.

"Um, I'm not sure what just happened," Garmadon admitted.

"Well, I'm going to find out!" Wu jogged ahead of his confused brother, in the direction the strange creature had gone.

The mist was thicker now, and Wu couldn't see anything in front of him but white mist. In his hurry, he forgot to look down at the path. He took a step . . .

And there was nothing beneath his feet! He plummeted off the mountain.

"Garmadon!" he yelled.

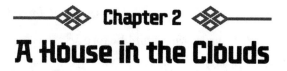

Chapter 2
A House in the Clouds

Garmadon ran toward his brother's voice, keeping his eyes on the path.

"Garmadon!"

Garmadon followed the sound to the edge of a ledge.

Oh no! Has Wu fallen off? he wondered. He dropped to his knees and looked over. Wu was gripping a rock just below the ledge, his legs dangling below him. Garmadon quickly grabbed Wu by the arms and pulled him up.

"Thanks," Wu said, his voice shaking a little. "That was a close one."

"You're welcome," Garmadon replied. "Just don't go running off again."

Wu brushed the dirt from his pants. "I had to find out what that weird creature was . . . and why it wanted us to follow it."

They headed back toward the path. Garmadon glanced at his brother.

I know he thanked me, but did he say anything about how good it was of me to save him? Garmadon wondered. *I mean, he and Father are convinced I'm turning evil. Would an evil guy bravely save his brother from plummeting into a deep abyss? Why doesn't anybody give me credit for the non-evil stuff that I do?*

"Follow me!" The half-monkey, half-dog creature appeared out of the fog again. He motioned for them to follow and headed along the path.

"OK, I definitely heard *that*," Garmadon said. "Let's find out what this mon-dog is up to!"

They followed the creature through the mist, making their way up to the top of the mountain. Finally, the clouds parted.

A flight of steps led to a white villa that stood on a platform supported by several tall pillars. The main house was made up of one large section covered by a curved roof, topped by a smaller, second section with another curved roof. Utility buildings, statues,

beautiful plants, and a vegetable garden surrounded the villa.

In front of the villa, a young woman stood at an easel, painting on a canvas. Her hair was dark purple, matching the scarf draped over her shoulder. She wore a garment the same color as the blue sky which the boys could now see. The ankle-length robe wrapped around her body and was held in place with a belt that matched the green grass at her feet.

The mon-dog ran up to her.

"Where have you been for so long, Balee?" she asked the creature. "I was worried."

"Boys! Boys!" the creature replied, and the girl turned to look. She raised an eyebrow.

"Are you two lost?" she asked.

"Hi, I'm Wu, and honestly, I'm not sure," Wu replied.

Wishy-washy Wu, Garmadon thought. "My name's Garmadon, and what my dear brother means is that we don't have *exact* directions to where we're going, but we're pretty sure we need to get over this mountain to get there."

The young woman smiled. "If you've climbed all the way up here, then you're probably tired and

hungry," she said. "I'm Peri. Why don't you come in? You're welcome to stay the night."

Garmadon and Wu exchanged glances and nodded. They'd been journeying long enough to know not to turn down food and shelter when they were offered.

Then Wu motioned toward the curious mon-dog. "Peri, what kind of animal is that? We've never seen one like it."

Peri grinned. "Balee is one of a kind," she answered. "My father . . . found him. He was always exploring this mountain, looking for new things to paint."

"I guess you take after your father, then," Garmadon said, nodding toward the easel, where Peri was painting a family of colorful birds in a tree.

Peri's smile faded. "I . . . I am trying."

She led the boys into the house, with Balee bouncing along at her side.

Garmadon and Wu hung back.

"Are we sure about this?" Wu whispered. "She's not really giving us straight answers. And her mood keeps changing."

"Relax, Wu," Garmadon said. "She met us only a minute ago. Maybe she's just shy."

Peri slid open the front door and they entered a large, airy room. The gleaming wood floor was splattered in places with drops of paint. There was no furniture, but a few easels stood scattered about, and several blank canvases were stacked up in a corner.

Large windows allowed sunlight to shine on the paintings on the walls, paintings bursting with bright color and beautiful creatures, like flowers, birds, and butterflies.

"Wow!" Wu exclaimed.

"My father painted most of these, but I am learning his craft," Peri explained.

"It will be nice to meet him," Wu said politely. "And the rest of your family."

"I'm alone," Peri said simply, and Garmadon felt a nudge from Wu. Peri turned away. "Come, let's get something to eat."

"Hungry! Hungry!" Balee said.

Peri smiled. "Don't worry, Balee. I'll feed you, too."

They followed Peri into a kitchen with more large windows, paintings of brightly colored vegetables on the walls, and more easels and half-painted canvases.

"How can we help?" Wu asked.

Peri picked up a bunch of carrots from a basket and tossed them to Wu. "Can you slice these, please?"

Garmadon grabbed them from his brother. "Let me," he said. He tossed a carrot into the air. Then he pulled out his sword and attacked the carrot with swift movements.

Ch-ch-ch-ch-ch.

He sliced up the carrot stick in seconds. Wu took off his hat and caught the pieces before they fell.

Peri laughed. "That's one way to slice a carrot," she said. "Just be sure not to slice up my canvases. They're works in progress."

"There's no danger of that, because I've been trained to wield this sword like a true master," Garmadon replied, slicing the rest of the bunch.

"Show-off," Wu whispered.

"Trained by whom?" Peri asked casually, but Garmadon noticed a look of interest in her eyes.

"By our father, the First Spinjitzu master," Garmadon answered, bragging a little. "Maybe you've heard of him?"

Peri looked thoughtful. "My father used to tell us stories of the great master who created the world of Ninjago using a special form of martial arts. He's your father? Wouldn't that make him, like, really old?"

"We're not exactly sure how old he is," Wu admitted.

Peri looked thoughtful again. "And you two are also masters of this . . . Spinjitzu?" she asked.

"We don't like to brag, but we're pretty good at it," Garmadon replied. "We could show you by mixing the salad, but that might not be a good idea."

"Garmadon exaggerates a little," Wu interjected. "Mastering the art of Spinjitzu is a journey with no end, as father would say. We're just ninja. There's still a lot for us to learn before we can call ourselves masters."

Peri smiled. "It's not every day that two ninja show up at my doorstep," she said, and patted Balee's head. "Good boy, Balee."

"Good boy! Good boy!"

Why is she praising Balee? Garmadon wondered. *Because we followed him here? She must be pretty lonely.*

Soon they were all seated around the kitchen table (except for Balee, who sat on top of it), eating a vegetable salad, chunks of chewy bread, and a potato soup that Peri had warmed up on the woodstove.

As they ate, Peri became less guarded, and asked the ninja questions about where they'd come from and where they were going. They explained that they had traveled a long way on a mission from their father.

"Why does your father want you to find the tea?" Peri asked, and Garmadon shot Wu a warning look. He hated when his brother told people the reason. It wasn't anyone's business but his.

Wu caught the look and shrugged. "Well, with Father, you don't ask questions. You just do what he says," Wu answered, which wasn't a lie. "Is your father like that, too?"

Peri stood up. "It's getting late," she said, and the friendly tone of her voice had vanished. "Let me show you to your room."

Garmadon and Wu looked at each other, and Garmadon shrugged as Peri hurried out of the kitchen.

"I think she's just not used to visitors," Garmadon whispered. "Socially awkward."

She led them down a hallway into a very clean room with two beds, a dresser, and bare white walls.

"I'm usually up early, but help yourself to tea in the morning if you're awake before I am," she said. Then she paused. "It's nice to have company. You two are welcome to stay for as long as you need."

"Well, actually, we have to—" Wu began, but Garmadon nudged him.

"That's a nice offer," Garmadon replied. "We'll think about it."

Peri smiled. "Good night, Wu and Garmadon!"

"Good night! Good night!" Balee echoed, and then Peri closed the door, leaving the brothers alone.

Wu plopped down on one of the beds. "All right, Garmadon, what's up? Is a pretty purple-haired girl blinding you to the fact that this place is weird? She has a talking monkey-dog for a pet and won't tell us what happened to her family!"

"I don't think this place is weird," Garmadon said, sitting down on the other bed. "It's beautiful here, and comfortable, and the food is good, so why not stay and rest up for a few days? It's a long way back down that mountain."

"That's for sure," Wu agreed. "But I just can't shake the feeling that something is wrong with all of this."

Garmadon yawned. "Get a good night's sleep, Wu. We'll figure it out in the morning."

Garmadon drifted off to sleep, where he dreamed of floating across a perfect blue sky on a fluffy purple cloud. A deep feeling of calm and peace came over him. Then he heard an eerie howl, and the sky in his dream turned black. Garmadon woke up with a start.

Aaaaaaoooooooooooooooooo!

I'm not dreaming anymore, he realized. *That howl is real!*

Garmadon darted out of bed and left his sleeping brother behind as he rushed into the hall. He made his way toward the sound.

Aaaaaaoooooooooooooooooo!

The sound came from behind a closed door. He reached out to open it—when it opened on its own! Peri stepped out and quickly closed it behind her.

"I—I heard something," Garmadon stammered.

"It's very windy up here on the mountain," Peri answered. She spoke quickly, avoiding his eyes. "Nothing to worry about. You should go back to your

room." Garmadon noticed she kept her back to the door and had not budged, almost as though she were blocking his way.

"Sure," Garmadon replied. "Good night, Peri."

That wasn't wind that I heard, Garmadon thought. *I hate to admit it, but Wu might be right. There's definitely something odd about this place, and maybe even our host, too.*

Chapter 3
Sights and Sounds

Garmadon and Wu woke at sunrise. Wu yawned and stretched.

"This is a very comfortable bed," Wu remarked. "Almost comfortable enough to make me spend another night here."

Garmadon almost told Wu about the strange howl he'd heard, and Peri's odd behavior behind that closed door. But he stopped himself. Part of him didn't want to give Wu the satisfaction that there was genuinely something weird about this place. The other part of him was curious. If there was something strange going on, he had an urge to find out what it was. Garmadon's curiosity won him over.

"See, nothing strange here at all," Garmadon said. "Just a soft mattress to sleep on and yummy food in our bellies." His stomach growled at the thought.

"I hate to admit it, but you might be right, brother," Wu said. "Let's have some breakfast and talk about our next move."

They found Peri on the balcony of the villa, which seemed to hang in the sky over the edge of the mountain. A table was set with tea and food, and Peri invited them to eat breakfast with her. They dined on bowls of creamy, warm porridge topped with strawberries as the morning sun shone overhead.

"I hope you've decided to stay," Peri said. "We don't often get visitors here. And honestly, I could use some help with the garden, if you don't mind."

Wu beamed. "Oh, I love plants," he said. "But tell me, Peri. You said you moved here with your family. Why are you all alone now?"

Peri took a deep breath, as though she was resolving to tell them the truth.

"My mother died three years ago," she said. "And then my father, and my sister . . . they left. But they'll be back."

As she turned away, Garmadon saw the sadness in her eyes.

"We can stay for a few days," he said, and Wu nodded in agreement.

Peri smiled. "That's wonderful! Thank you both so much."

"Hello! Hello!"

The little mon-dog swung up onto the balcony and jumped into Peri's lap.

"Good news, Balee," Peri said. "Wu and Garmadon are going to stay for a few days."

Balee looked at the brothers and his eyes got wide.

"Beware! Beware!" he chattered.

Wu raised an eyebrow. "Is he like a parrot, just saying words at random, or does he understand what he says?"

"He understands, but he's just being silly right now," Peri said, wagging a finger at Balee. "Don't be teasing our guests, Balee. They're going to help us."

Balee nodded. "OK! OK!" Then he hopped off Peri's lap onto the table and slurped down the porridge she'd set out for him.

"So, what do you grow in your garden?" Wu asked.

"Just about everything we eat," Peri replied. "But it takes up a lot of time, and I like to save the afternoons for painting. Come on, I'll show you."

They left the balcony and walked back through the main room, its walls full of paintings. The brothers couldn't help noticing how bright and happy the colors were. A blue waterfall flowed into a stream winding through trees with orange and yellow leaves. White swans floated in a shimmering blue lake with pink lilies. Giant red mushrooms with white spots grew in a forest filled with equally giant flowers.

"I'd love to take a closer look at these paintings while we're here," Wu said.

"Sure, there'll be time for that," Peri remarked.

Garmadon glanced at the painting nearest to him. Green ducks flew across a dark blue lake, their wings flapping. . . .

Garmadon blinked. It looked as though the ducks were moving, their wings actually flapping.

"The ducks!" he blurted out, pointing. "They're moving!"

Peri smiled. "That shows you what kind of artist my father was. His paintings are so realistic they almost seem alive. Come on, let me show you the garden!"

Garmadon looked at the painting again. The ducks were still. Wu approached him. "What's the matter, brother? You're as pale as a ghost."

"Nothing. Must be that mountain air," Garmadon replied, and they followed Peri outside.

She led them to a clearing on the south side of the villa, a flat patch of land that wasn't terribly big, but filled with green, growing plants. Garmadon counted ten rows of vegetables. Berry bushes and pear trees bordered the garden in the back, and a well sat in the center. A wooden wheelbarrow leaned against a stone garden wall.

Peri grabbed two wicker baskets and handed them to Wu and Garmadon.

"We need to pick all the blackberries before the birds get them," she explained, and picked up a basket for herself. "Then we can work on weeding."

"I'm *berry* happy to help," Wu joked, and Garmadon groaned.

"Maybe you should help pick the corn, brother," Garmadon said. "Because that was really corny."

Wu grinned. "Good one, Garmadon."

They got to work. Garmadon soon found that berry picking required patience and care, unlike slicing carrots in midair.

"I bet I can fill my basket before you can," Garmadon challenged Wu.

"Bet you can't!" Wu said, and the ninja began to pick berries at a frantic pace.

"Don't squish them!" Peri warned. "Now, you've got to tell me about some of these exciting adventures you've had."

The boys talked as they worked. They told Peri stories about training with Nineko, the enchanted cat ninja, and defeating an evil puppet master named Tanabrax and his minions. Garmadon was explaining how he had saved his brother from being stuck in a puppet body forever when Wu cried out.

"Done! I win!" Wu yelled.

Garmadon looked at his brother's basket, which was filled to the top with berries. His own was almost filled, but not quite.

"Not fair!" Garmadon protested. "Balee's been swiping berries from mine."

"Swipe! Swipe!" Balee laughed, and he grabbed a handful of berries from Garmadon's basket.

"That was a close one," Peri said. "Hey, Garmadon, I bet you can win the weeding contest."

That was all Garmadon needed to hear.

"Ninjaaaaago!"

Garmadon launched into Spinjitzu and whirled through the vegetable beds, pulling out the weeds. When he finished, a pile of weeds was stacked high in the wheelbarrow.

"You didn't even give me a chance," Wu grumbled.

"So that's Spinjitzu," Peri said. "Impressive. This is all a really big help. I wish you both could stay forever."

Forever. The way she said it sent a chill up Garmadon's spine, and he wasn't sure why.

I've got to figure out what's going on with Peri, he thought. *And something tells me I'd better do it soon!*

Chapter 4
Trapped!

Wu and Garmadon spent the rest of the morning helping Peri in the garden, and then they all had lunch together.

I'm glad Garmadon was right, Wu thought. *It's good to rest in a place where there are no monsters to fight and the host isn't an evil villain in disguise.*

"This is delicious, Peri," he said. "Thanks so much for inviting us to stay."

"You can both relax this afternoon while I paint," Peri told them. "Unless . . . No, it's asking too much."

"What is it?" Wu asked.

"Well, I was wondering if I could paint you both?" Peri asked. "I'm running out of things to paint up here. And Balee doesn't like to sit still."

"Busy Balee!" the mon-dog agreed.

Wu and Garmadon looked at each other. Wu shrugged. "I think we can sit still for a while. It would be cool to be in a painting, right, Garmadon?"

"Sure, why not?" Garmadon asked. "When we're famous ninja someday, you can hang it in a museum."

Wu shook his head. "Us? Famous? Like that would ever happen."

Outside, Peri set up her easel and paints in front of a small boulder on the edge of the woods.

"Do you think you could pose in a fighting stance on top of that rock?" Peri asked. "Maybe using your weapons? That might look awesome."

"We can give it a try," Wu said. He jumped onto the boulder in one leap and stood with his feet apart. Then he gripped his staff with both hands and held it in front of him in a defensive position.

Garmadon jumped up onto the rock next to Wu. He posed with a triumphant smile, raising his sword over his head.

"Perfect, if you can hold it!" Peri said, and she dipped her paintbrush into the paint and began.

"Staying here is a good idea, Garmadon," Wu remarked. "I feel kind of silly now, being worried."

Garmadon lowered his voice to a whisper, and Wu thought he saw a guilty look on his brother's face. "Listen, Wu, I think you might have been on to something when you said this place was weird. Last night, I heard a strange sound."

Garmadon quickly explained his encounter with Peri the night before.

Wu's eyes widened. "Why didn't you tell me? And what are we still doing here?"

"We're ninja," Garmadon replied. "I don't think we're in any danger we can't handle. And I'm really curious to know what's going on with Peri. Aren't you curious?"

Wu glanced at the purple-haired girl, who was concentrating on her canvas.

"I am," he said. "But when we're done here, we should start investigating. I'd like to know what's behind that locked door you saw Peri protecting."

Peri painted and painted some more. The boys held their poses, but it grew more and more difficult to stay still. Wu started humming and whistling, and Garmadon snapped at him to stop.

"Come on Wu, remember our Spinjitzu training," he said. "Father has put us through a lot more than this. Close your eyes. Focus on your breath."

Wu nodded and closed his eyes. Then the sun got brighter and hotter, and despite their best efforts, the two brothers started to yawn.

Wu felt himself drifting off to sleep, and he struggled to stay awake. He fell down on one knee. Garmadon was already curled up on his side, napping.

"Sorry," he mumbled. "Just need to close my eyes for a minute . . ."

When he opened his eyes again, he found Garmadon sitting upright, looking around in wonder. Wu gazed from left to right.

They were still standing on a rock, but they weren't on the mountain anymore, and Peri and her easel were nowhere in sight. A waterfall flowed behind them into a sparkling blue stream. Bright purple and orange flowers grew along the stream's banks. The scene, and the colors, reminded Wu of something. . . .

"Does this look familiar?" he asked. "Garmadon, where are we?"

Garmadon turned and gasped. Wu spun around.

Peri's face, enormous as the trees, floated in the air in front of them.

"I'm sorry," she said. "I had to be sure you would help me."

Then her face disappeared.

Wu's mind raced. *She's big, and we're small. She was painting us, and now we're in a different place with bright colors.*

"Peri has trapped us inside a painting!" he cried, and Garmadon said the words at the same time.

"I was right about this all along!" Wu yelled, although he knew anger and fear weren't going to help them right now. "I guess we're destined to fall into the clutches of deceitful foes wherever we go. There's nothing we can do now except try to solve this problem."

"If we're inside a painting, then maybe we can get out," Garmadon suggested. *"Ninjaaaaaago!"*

Garmadon launched into Spinjitzu and hurled himself off the boulder, in the direction where they had seen Peri's face. Wu watched his brother spin right into some kind of invisible force field and bounce back.

Maybe it'll take two of us, Wu thought.

"Ninjaaago!" He jumped and joined his brother, spinning like a tornado into the force field.

wHOMP!

He felt himself collide with the field as it pushed him back. But he didn't give up, and neither did Garmadon.

wHOMP! wHOMP! wHOMP!

They crashed into the force field again and again, with no results. Finally, they slowed down and collapsed in the soft green grass.

"Well, this is definitely a problem," Wu said.

"Definitely," Garmadon agreed. "But we'll find a way out."

"Don't bother," said a voice behind them. "There's no way out of here."

The boys turned to see a large white deer with sparkling blue eyes standing there. Her crystal antlers glittered.

"Another talking animal?" Garmadon asked.

"I am Jelena," she said. "And there is something you must know: Peri has sent you in here to fight a monster!"

Chapter 5
Jeleña's Tale

Wu's head was spinning. There was so much to figure out. How had Peri trapped them inside a painting? Who was this magical-looking white deer? And what did she mean about a monster?

Jelena looked at the brothers with sympathy. She seemed to understand their confusion.

"This is a lot to explain," she said. "Please, sit and listen. I have a tale to tell."

"A good one, I hope," Garmadon grumbled.

Jelena thought for a while. "Once upon a time, there was a magician whose name was Mindaro," she said. "He channeled all of his magic into one very special talent: he could create paintings that came to life."

"Aha!" Garmadon blurted out. "I thought I saw ducks moving in one of his paintings. Now I know it was real!"

Jelena nodded. "Yes, exactly. Mindaro was a gentle man, and he created paintings to delight and entertain those around him. He worried that too much natural beauty was disappearing from the world of Ninjago, and he wanted to preserve it.

"Mindaro married a woman named Violet, and they had two daughters, Periwinkle and Indigo—Peri and Indi for short."

Peri mentioned she had a sister, Wu thought.

"Seeking a peaceful place to create his magical art, Mindaro moved his family to the top of a mountain in the middle of Ninjago," Jelena continued. "He painted scenes of enchanted forests and beautiful landscapes, and populated them with wondrous creatures, like myself, to delight his wife and daughters."

"Wait, Mindaro *created* you?" Garmadon asked.

"Yes," Jelena applied. "In many ways, he is like a father to me, and Peri and . . . Indi are like . . . my sisters. They spent many happy hours in front of this painting, watching me frolic and play. I longed to leave my painting and enter the world with my sisters, and Mindaro listened and tried to create magic that would let me do so. He began with Balee."

Wu gasped. "Balee? Started out as a painting?"

Jelena nodded. "Yes. He is smaller and simpler than I, and Mindaro was able to bring him into the real world. I eagerly waited my turn. But then . . . everything changed.

"The girls' mother, Violet, became ill and died quite suddenly. Mindaro was overcome with despair. He would not eat, or sleep, or paint. His daughters urged him to paint again, thinking it might bring him joy. He reluctantly agreed. But he did not have the heart to use bright colors and painted in only gray and black and white. When Peri and Indi asked him why, he said that those colors represented his sadness.

"As he painted, his grief and anger overtook him. His magic was so powerful that storm clouds appeared in the sky over the mountain. Peri and Indi begged him to stop, but Mindaro kept painting, as though some mighty force had overtaken him. His creation took the form of a monster, a huge monster with no color or joy."

Wu shuddered. "But wait, if he painted things that came to life, does that mean that the monster also came to life?"

"It did, and to Mindaro's surprise, this monster had evil powers beyond his imagination. Mindaro's magic had become so strong that the monster was just as powerful, and it tried to escape from the painting!" Jelena said.

"And I'm guessing the monster isn't a cute little creature like Balee," Garmadon interjected.

"Indeed it is not," Jelena replied. "The monster is huge and hideous. Mindaro attempted to stop it, but the monster dragged him inside, along with Indi, who clung to her father's robe to save him. Before the monster could grab Peri, Mindaro used magic to contain the monster inside the painting, which meant that he and Indi were contained, too."

"So, Peri was saved, while her sister became trapped," Wu said, slowly. He glanced at his brother.

I know how that feels, he thought. *On that day in the monastery, years ago, when I lost my katana, I was too afraid to retrieve it. But Garmadon jumped over the wall to get it for me, and got bitten by the snake that may have infected him with evil,*

as Father suspects. I often wonder what would have happened if
I had been the one to get bitten that day. . . .

Garmadon spoke up, interrupting Wu's thoughts. "And you're saying that Mindaro and Indi have been trapped ever since their mother died three years ago?"

"Yes, and they will remain trapped there forever unless someone can save them," Jelena explained. "Mindaro is using powerful magic to keep the monster, which he calls the Chroma, inside the painting. That means that he and Indi cannot leave, either, unless someone rescues them."

"Do you mean it's possible to travel inside the painting?" Wu asked.

"We can travel into any of Mindaro's paintings, including the Chroma," Jelena replied. "But once inside the Chroma painting, no one can leave until the Chroma is defeated."

Garmadon's eyes lit up. "Wait, is that why Peri painted *us* inside a painting?" he asked. "So that we'd go fight the Chroma? Why didn't she just ask us?"

Jelena shook her head sadly. "Peri and I still talk every day. Peri is filled with guilt that her sister is trapped, and she is free. She has spent the last three years trying to learn her father's magic to help free Mindaro and

Indi. She has learned to bring characters to life in her paintings. First, she tried painting warriors and sorcerers, but she told me that those painted heroes all failed, swallowed by the Chroma."

"Then Peri became more and more desperate. She discovered how to trap real people and creatures inside paintings," Jelena continued.

"We should have guessed," Wu said. "But she seemed so nice."

"She's not a bad person, I swear," Jelena replied. "But despair has made her do bad things. She resorted to trickery by inviting anyone who came to the mountain to stay. Then she painted them into a painting so I could explain to them what needs to be done before facing the Chroma. A pirate, an explorer, a warrior, a winged lion and more—she sent them all in here, knowing that they would have to try to defeat the Chroma if they ever wanted to be free."

Jelena looked away sadly. "I am sorry for my part in all of this, but I do not know how to stop Peri. And I have been too frightened to venture into the Chroma painting myself."

"What happened to everyone who Peri sent to fight the Chroma?" Wu asked, but he felt like he knew the answer.

The white deer looked into his eyes. "The Chroma swallowed those brave enough to fight it, just like the ones Peri had painted herself before," she replied. "I know there's no way I can possibly defeat the monster, which is why I stay here. And as for why she didn't just ask you, Garmadon, it's because she is too afraid you would refuse. She is desperate to reunite with her father and sister, and will do anything to make it happen."

Wu and Garmadon were silent for a minute, taking it all in.

"You're sure there's no other way for us to get out of here?" Wu asked finally.

Jelena shook her head. "No. Of course, you don't have to fight the Chroma. You could stay here in this painting. It's quite beautiful. But Peri told me she was impressed by your ninja skills and thought that you two might be able to succeed, where others have not."

"I'm not afraid of some big old angry paint blob," Garmadon said. "We're ninja, and we've faced tons of scary monsters and taught them a lesson. We're going to find this thing and defeat it, right, Wu?"

Garmadon's confidence gave Wu a boost of energy.

"Right! Let's get this Chroma!" he cried, and ran a few steps before he stopped. "Uh, Jelena, which way to the Chroma's painting?"

"We'll get there the way I got here. Follow me," the deer said mysteriously, and she turned and galloped off into the field of flowers.

Wu and Garmadon ran after her until she reached the edge of the meadow. Suddenly, a portal swirled in the blue sky.

"Jump!" Jelena cried, and she leapt into the portal and disappeared.

Chapter 6
From Painting to Painting

Garmadon and Wu ran toward the portal and leapt into it, too, side by side.

A strange feeling, like a jolt of static electricity, passed through the brothers as they moved through the portal. It spit them out on the other side, and they tumbled into a forest. Giant flowers towered over their heads, and nearby, a large willow tree's branches danced in the cool breeze. The forest floor was dotted with tiny blue and white flowers. And enormous red and white mushroom towered over them.

"I recognize this painting!" Garmadon cried. "It's in the main room of the villa."

Jelena looked around and brightened.

"This is the painting that Mindaro created when he made me," Jelena explained.

Wu gazed around. "It's beautiful. Do any other creatures live here?"

"Well, there's Will," Jelena said, darting her head back and forth from time to time. "But really we should keep moving we—"

Suddenly a man with a curly mustache streaked past them, wearing a white, belted smock and red pants.

"Run! Intruders!" he cried. Then he jumped behind the mushroom and peeked out. "Jelena, get to safety!"

"Relax, Will," Jelena said. "This is Wu and Garmadon. Peri painted them into a painting."

Will stepped out from behind the mushroom. "Sorry to hear that. I assume you'll be like the others, and foolishly take on this impossible task."

"Of course we will! We're ninja!" Garmadon cried. He looked Will up and down. "And what are *you*, exactly?"

"Well, that's the thing," Will replied. "I am but a simple traveling barber. I got lost on Peri's mountain and Balee led me to her. I was very frightened, and as we talked I told Balee I was a worrier, but he heard 'warrior,' and he relayed that to Peri and—well, here I am. I have no intention of fighting that foul beast. Jelena's painting is quite comfortable, and we've become the best of friends, haven't we?"

"Yeah, sure," Jelena replied, but she turned to the brothers and mouthed the word "no." "Anyway, we've got to get going. See you later, Will."

"Good luck, ninja! You're going to need it!" Will called out. Then he pulled a pair of scissors from his smock pocket. "If you change your minds, I'm happy to take care of those shaggy hairstyles for you. For a discount, of course."

Jelena galloped off to the edge of the magical forest, and the brothers followed. As the trees thinned, she came to another portal.

"Does this lead to the Chroma's painting?" Wu asked.

"No," Jelena replied. "We must pass through several different paintings to get there. I know the way. But stay alert. Not all of the paintings are as safe as this one."

"What do you mean?" Wu asked, but Jelena had already jumped through the portal. With a shrug, the brothers followed.

The boys landed in the painting and gazed around. Jelena faced them. They were standing in a field of bright green grass with large, uneven stalks. A single flower grew in the field. It was very tall, with red petals, and a smiling face inside its pink center.

"It's hot in here," Garmadon remarked. He looked up to see a giant, yellow sun hanging low in the sky.

Rough lines extended from the main circle of the sun. It looked strangely familiar, somehow. . . .

"Did a child paint this?" Wu asked.

"Peri painted it, when she was younger," Jelena said. "It was the first time she realized she had the same magic as her father. Now come, we must get to the next portal before—"

"Friends!"

The brothers turned to see a giant stomp toward them—a giant that looked like a purple stick figure with purple hair.

"That's Peri's self-portrait," the white deer explained. "If she grabs you, she won't let go. Now come, quickly!"

The green ground trembled under their feet as they ran from the painted stick figure that had come to life.

"Friends! Friends! Come play!" the stick figure yelled. She reached for them with her purple stick hands. Luckily, they had reached the next portal.

"This part's tricky," Jelena said. "When you go through the portal, grab on to the first one you see."

"First one what?" Wu asked, but Jelena was already through the portal.

That electric tingle jolted them again, but this time, they didn't land on a smooth surface.

They fell! Then . . . *whoosh!* An enormous, beautiful butterfly swooped past Garmadon, and he remembered, *Grab on to the first one you see.* He reached for the butterfly's fuzzy back and pulled himself on. Then he straddled it like he would a horse.

"Wu!" he yelled. Had his brother figured it out, too, or had he fallen into some kind of magical abyss?

"Garmadon!" Wu cried. He was perched on a butterfly with pale yellow wings, zigzagging around the sky. "Do you think these butterflies are going to sprout fangs and try to bite us or something?"

Garmadon steadied himself and studied the painting. Giant butterflies fluttered around a pale blue sky. The butterflies were detailed and very realistic-looking.

"I think they're just normal butterflies!" Garmadon yelled back, and he grinned as his butterfly zigzagged joyfully across the painting, too.

I think I saw this painting in the villa, he thought.

Then Jelena flew up to them. Colorful wings had sprouted from her back!

"Good job!" she said. "This is Mindaro's painting, and it's beautiful, but quite tricky. Basically you have to wait until your butterfly gets close enough to a portal to jump."

"Can't we sprout wings, like you did?" Wu asked.

Jelena shook her head. "Nope. Mindaro made me a magical deer, and I can do a few tricks, like sprout wings when I need them. It comes in handy. But you two will be fine. Come on!"

Jelena flew away from them. Garmadon's butterfly made a loop in the air, and he wrapped his arm's more tightly around its neck.

"Come on, follow that flying deer!" he urged.

He heard Wu shouting at his butterfly, too.

"To the left! To the left! Please, no more loops! *Aaaahhhhhh!*"

The butterflies looped and swirled and fluttered, and the ninja couldn't control them. But eventually,

they got near the portal just as Jelena passed through. Garmadon saw Wu leap off his butterfly and into the portal, his arms and legs flailing.

"Here goes nothing," Garmadon said. Gripping the butterfly's neck, he stood up. The insect's body lurched under his feet and started to fly away.

"Aahhhhhhhhhhhhhh!" Garmadon launched himself from the butterfly's back and dove into the portal.

wHOMP!

He traveled through it and landed on . . . a large pile of gold coins?

"What the—?" he began, but Wu and Jelena both shushed him. Puzzled, Garmadon stood up and followed their gaze.

They were inside a large cave, where an enormous dragon slept on top of the pile of coins and other golden treasures. The dragon's orangey-red scales rippled as the dragon breathed, and glimmered under the cave's torchlight.

"We need to be very quiet," Jelena whispered. "We have to get past the dragon to reach the portal."

"What kind of dragon is this, anyway?" Wu whispered. "Real dragons do not care for gold and treasures. Our father taught us that real dragons are not greedy. They care for something entirely different."

"Mindaro painted this from an old fairy tale," Jelena explained. "It's called *Guardian of Your Heart's Treasure.*"

"Why doesn't Peri just sic this dragon on the Chroma?" Garmadon whispered back.

"Peri can't control the dragon, because her father painted it," Jelena explained. "One time I tried to wake it up and well . . . I'm lucky I got away with just a scorched tail."

They tiptoed across the heaping mounds of treasure, moving as quietly as they could. Soon they reached the dragon's head. Steam escaped from the dragon's nostrils with every breath.

Garmadon saw the portal spinning just beyond the dragon's head. Jelena jumped through. Wu lined up to leap into the portal, but at that moment Garmadon spotted a golden urn half-buried in the coins. He could make out the words NORTHERN COAST and TEA.

"Hey Wu, it's the tea!" Garmadon yelled, and dove for the urn. "Yaaay!"

"Garmadon, shhhhhhh!" Wu warned.

But it was too late. The dragon's eyes opened, and so did its huge mouth. Garmadon saw flames sparking deep inside the dragon's throat.

"Garmadon, run!" Wu yelled.

Garmadon quickly grabbed the urn and felt the heat of the dragon's breath as he charged ahead, where Wu was waiting for him.

Roooooooooaaaaaaaaaar!

Fiery dragon breath licked at their heels as the brothers hurtled through the portal. This time, they landed on the wooden deck of a ship, in the middle of a rainstorm.

Garmadon got to his feet. "Thanks for waiting for me back there, Wu," he said.

"Sure, but what were you thinking? That was dangerous," Wu said.

Garmadon held out the urn. "But I got the tea, see? We can go home after we take down the Chroma."

Wu looked at the urn and frowned. "Did you read it?" he asked.

"Sure. What do you mean?" Garmadon said, and he turned the urn to face him. Now he could see the letters covered up by the coins: NORTHERN COAST TEAM CHAMPIONS. His heart sank. "Oh. It's just a trophy."

"Hey guys, in case you didn't notice, we're in the middle of a storm," Jelena interrupted. "Quick, take down the sails! Then somebody needs to grab the ship's wheel. It can't be me, because I can't do it with my hooves."

"Uh, sure!" Garmadon said, trying to get his bearings. Jumping from painting to painting was leaving him dazed and confused. But now he realized that the ship they'd landed on was in the middle of the ocean, and the rain was part of a terrible storm—a beautiful, colorful storm. Bright yellow lightning streaked the dark purple sky, and the ocean water churned in shades of deep blue and green.

Garmadon and Wu ran to the mast. The white fabric sails flapped violently in the wind, and the brothers, who had some experience sailing, grabbed the ropes and pulled down the sails. The boat rocked as they worked, and waves lapped onto the deck as rain poured down, splashing them.

Then they ran to the ship's wheel. Jelena stood next to it, gazing into the darkness up ahead.

"The next portal's not far, but if we don't steer toward it, we'll never get there," she said. "Steady our course as best you can."

Garmadon and Wu gripped the wheel together, bracing themselves against the howling wind. The ship careened forward, and Garmadon's stomach lurched.

Then, suddenly, a swirling portal appeared in the air in front of them.

"Garmadon, Wu, use the rope to help you, and go!" Jelena yelled over the wind. "That portal leads to the

Chroma! It will lead you into the painting, but there is no way out once you go through. After that, you're on your own."

"Will you be OK?" Wu yelled.

"Don't worry about me," Jelena said, as her two wings appeared on her back. "Defeat that Chroma once and for all! If you brave ninja can't do it, I fear nobody can."

Jelena flew off into the storm, and the brothers stared at the portal. They picked up the long rope attached to the ship's mast. Then they took a deep breath.

"We can do this," Wu said, trying to stay confident.

"Yeah, let's get this Chroma!" Garmadon added.

Then, gripping the rope, they swung into the portal.

Chapter 7
The Grays

The brothers landed in a world with a flat, gray landscape with nothing but rocks and caves jutting from the dull ground. In the distance sat a dark, gloomy fog. The force of their jump caused the long rope to snap at its base and pool at their feet.

It was eerily quiet after the noise of the ocean storm, and a small shiver of fear crept up Garmadon's spine.

"This place is creepy," he remarked.

Wu agreed. "You can say that again," he said, looking around. "You know, we don't know much about this painting, or where to find the Chroma."

"I have a feeling it won't be hard to find," Garmadon said. "We might as well just start walking."

Before they could take a step, the ground erupted in a circle around them. Figures rose up, the same color as the gray ground. Each one had a gray, human-looking body with two arms, two legs, and a head. None had a nose or a mouth—just two empty cracks where

their eyes should be. The creepy creatures surrounded Garmadon and Wu.

They both jumped into a ninja stance, ready to battle.

"What are these? Baby Chromas?" Wu asked.

"No idea," Garmadon replied. "Jelena didn't warn us about these. But I'm guessing they're not friendly."

Then, without a word, the gray creatures charged forward. Both brothers jumped up and over the attackers, landing outside the circle.

BAM!

The creatures crashed into each other.

"Looks like these Grays are solid," Wu remarked. "That means . . ."

"Time for some ninja moves!" Garmadon cried. He slashed at the nearest Gray with his katana, separating it into two halves. The two pieces seemed to melt back

into the gray ground, and then two more Grays rose
in its place.

"Oh, it's going to be like that, is it?" Garmadon
asked, as the two new Grays launched themselves
at him. He jumped over their heads and landed,
somersaulting. He popped up next to Wu as his
brother whacked a Gray with his staff. The creature
fell back, melting back into the ground, and another
two popped up.

"This could go on forever," Wu remarked.

"Unless . . ." Garmadon said as he picked up
the long rope they had brought with them from the
painting of the ship.

Wu grinned. *"Ninjaaaaaago!"*

The brothers launched into Spinjitzu, whirling around the Grays like human tornados. They circled the creatures spinning faster and faster, wrapping the rope around them. When Wu and Garmadon stopped spinning, the army of Grays were stuck into what looked like a giant ball of yarn.

"Great thinking, Garmadon!" Wu said, and the two ninja slapped their palms together in victory.

Rooooraaaaaaaaaaaaaaar!

They spun around at the sound of an angry, unearthly howl. Then both boys gasped.

The creature the size of a small mountain moved swiftly across the barren land. At first, it looked like a mass of swirling, gray fog, but then its details became clear. Two arms with ghostly fingers reached for them. Two black eyes glowed in the top of its head, and a huge mouth opened up, revealing a black hole with long, gray teeth.

Wu's eyes widened. "The Chroma," he said. "We need a strategy."

"We have Spinjitzu. That's our strategy," Garmadon shot back.

The Chroma raced closer, reaching for them with its long, gray arms.

Garmadon nodded to Wu. "Ready? *Ninjaaaaa—*"

There is no hope.

Garmadon froze. He heard the voice inside his brain, a deep, growling voice that filled his soul with despair. And somehow he knew that the voice was the Chroma's.

All is lost. There is no point in continuing your journey, because nothing will change.

Why is he talking to me? Garmadon wondered. *Is he talking to Wu, too? Or is this like when Nineko picked me to be her minion instead of Wu, or when the Sphinx tormented me in her maze?*

Nothing will change, the Chroma repeated. *You are who you are, Garmadon.*

Deep in his bones, Garmadon knew the Chroma was right. When he wasn't pretending everything was fine, he could feel the evil inside him, like a poisonous ball in the pit of his stomach. No tea was going to cure him. He knew it. Wu had hope, but why? What was the point of—

He felt his brother grab him by the arm, and Wu's voice sounded like it was far away.

"Garmadon, snap out of it! We've got to run!"

Chapter 8
The Magician's Cave

Wu had been ready to launch into Spinjitzu when he saw his brother freeze. Garmadon had a haunted look in his eyes, one Wu had never seen before. He just stared at the Chroma as it got closer and closer.

Yelling at his brother seemed to do the trick.

"Garmadon!" Wu said again. "Let's go!"

Garmadon blinked and snapped out of his trance. The two of them raced across the barren landscape as fast as they could.

"What happened back there?" Wu asked.

"I heard the Chroma inside my head!" Garmadon yelled back. "Didn't you?"

ROOOOOOOORAAAAAAR!

If we don't find shelter, we'll have to fight, Wu thought. *But what if Garmadon freezes up again? What did he mean about hearing the Chroma inside his head?*

Then Wu spotted something—a dim light glowing through the fog. He ran toward it, and Garmadon followed.

"Quickly!" A woman's voice called to them from the light.

ROOOOOOOARRRRRR!

Wu and Garmadon took one last, long leap toward the light. They tumbled into a cave glowing with light from torches on the walls. A young woman with pale lavender hair worn in a braid looked at them and sighed.

"Don't worry, the Chroma can't come in here," she said. Then she raised her voice. "Father, Peri has sent more warriors!"

A voice grunted in response from a corner of the cave, where a man with a bushy beard was painting strange symbols on the cave wall. His face looked tired, and he did not respond to his daughter.

"You must be Indi and Mindaro," Wu said. "Yes, Peri did send us. I'm Wu, and this is my brother, Garmadon."

"Well, technically she sent us. She didn't really *ask* us, but here we are," Garmadon pointed out.

"I am so sorry," Indi said. "We know that she uses trickery to do this, and we are very sorry. Peri feels so much guilt that she escaped the Chroma's clutches that she has resorted to dishonesty in her desperation. But that is not the girl she is at heart. I urge you, stay here with us in this cave where it is safe. There is no way for you to defeat the Chroma."

"We *will* defeat the Chroma!" Garmadon blurted out. Wu nodded.

Indi raised an eyebrow. "Oh really?" she asked. "Because you were just running away from it right now, weren't you?"

Garmadon shrugged. "That's because we need to strategize."

"Hey, that's what *I* said," Wu objected.

Indi sighed. "Then you are foolish, like all of the others. And I will not be able to stop you."

"What's our choice?" Garmadon asked. "If we don't fight the Chroma, we'll be stuck here in this cave with you and your father. I mean, you seem nice and everything, but this place is a little, well, dark."

"Better to be alive and gloomy than swallowed by the Chroma," Indi replied.

Wu glanced over at Mindaro, who continued to paint symbols on the cave wall. "What's he doing?"

"It is a magic spell," Indi replied. "My father must paint these walls every day to keep the Chroma trapped in this world. He is very weak, because it takes every ounce of his energy to keep the Chroma here. It is why he rarely speaks."

"Can't he use his magic to bust us all out of here?" Garmadon explained.

Indi shook her head. "No. That might release the Chroma into the world. It's too risky."

"So, if we defeat the Chroma, your father can use his magic to get us out?" Wu asked.

"Yes, but as I've told you, it's impossible," she said. "My sister, Peri, has sent many brave and strong warriors here to help us, and they failed. And to be honest, you don't look more powerful than any who have gone before you."

Garmadon looked at her. "Oh yeah? Were any of them the ninja sons of the First Spinjitzu Master?"

Indi raised an eyebrow. "No," she admitted.

Wu paced back and forth, thinking. "Indi, ninja don't back down from a challenge. We are going to fight the Chroma. Can you tell us anything that might help us? First of all, who are those little Gray guys?"

"The Chroma created them, as a first line of defense," she explained. "And the Chroma can make

new ones whenever it chooses. They always come in large numbers. If we venture outside this cave, they are the first to attack."

"And what about the Chroma? What happens when you try to fight it?" Garmadon asked.

Indi frowned. "The Chroma is a huge mass of despair and anger. You can't punch it or kick it into submission. When it gets close to you, it swallows you. There is no way to fight it."

"Every opponent we've ever faced has had a weakness," Garmadon told her. "We just have to find the Chroma's."

"Right!" Wu said. "What is the way to defeat despair and anger?"

Then the brothers looked at one another.

"Joy!" Wu cried.

"Happiness!" answered Garmadon.

"There is no joy or happiness here," Indi said. "Only gray sadness."

Gray sadness. Wu thought about the gray landscape of the Chroma painting. Then he remembered the beauty of Jelena's enchanted forest. He thought about soft, green grass, purple and orange flowers, and the blue, sparkling stream.

"Color!" he cried. "We can fight the Chroma with bright, happy colors!"

Garmadon nodded. "Exactly! It's all about balance. Like Father says, 'When something is off, everything falls.'" he said. "But, um, how exactly would using bright colors work to defeat the Chroma?"

Then Mindaro turned to them, and spoke in a hoarse, tired voice.

"There is no hope, ninja," he said. "The only color in this world is what Indi and I brought with us, and there is precious little left."

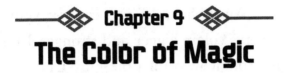

Chapter 9
The Color of Magic

Garmadon pointed to the torches in the cave, crackling with orange and yellow flame.

"There's color," he pointed out. "How did that get here?"

"I created them with the last splatters of paint on my clothing," Mindaro replied, looking down at his paint-stained robe. "But no more color remains."

Wu shook his head. "What about Peri?" he asked. "She added us to Jelena's painting. Can't she add color to this one?"

Mindaro was silent for a moment. "I have thought about it, but there is no way to ask that of Peri. She can watch what happens in this painting, but we cannot speak to her unless we travel to the front of the painting. And we risk being swallowed by the Chroma before we get to her. Then the problem remains: how would we use the colors to defeat the monster?"

"Like my brother Garmadon always says, we've got Spinjitzu," Wu replied. "If you can use your magic to make Peri's colors bigger and stronger, I think we could use Spinjitzu to turn the gray Chroma into a candy-colored cloud."

Mindaro sighed. "My magic is so weak. I don't know if I have enough to make Peri's colors strong enough to overtake the Chroma."

Indi grabbed her father by the shoulders. "You have to try, Father!" she said. "This is the first real hope we've had in three years."

Mindaro shook his head. "It is too risky. If the Chroma gets out . . ."

"You said so yourself, your magic is weakening," Indi shot back. "The Chroma will get out eventually . . . unless we take action."

She grabbed a torch from the wall. "Now is the time!"

"Yes!" Garmadon cheered.

Wu looked at Indi. "How far is it to the front of the painting?"

"Not far," she said. "If you and Garmadon can keep the Chroma and the Grays at bay, I can talk to Peri. Father just needs to let down the magical shield."

"I can only do so for a short time," Mindaro said. "If there is a chance the Chroma will escape, I must close it."

"We won't let the Chroma escape," Garmadon promised. "Come on, let's go!"

Indi and Mindaro moved to the front of the cave, but Wu held Garmadon back.

"Garmadon, you said you heard the Chroma's voice in your head before," he said. "Are you going to be OK? We can't have you freezing up again."

Garmadon scowled. "I'm not going to fail, all right? You don't need to worry about me."

How can he be so sure? Wu wondered. *I wish I could figure out what's going on with Garmadon, but there's no time. We just have to try and see what happens.*

He nodded. "OK."

They joined Indi and Mindaro at the cave entrance.

"Father, how fast can you run?" Indi asked.

"As fast as my weak body will allow," Mindaro replied. "But I will do my best."

The four of them left the cave, jogging quickly. Indi and Mindaro headed toward a pale light in the distance, across the gray landscape.

Immediately, Grays began to pop up. Wu wasn't sure if they were the same ones he and Garmadon had tied up, or new ones. But it didn't matter.

SLAM!

Wu knocked one down with his staff.

BAM!

Garmadon twirled, taking one down with a swift, round kick.

Just like before, two more Grays popped up when each one fell.

Garmadon groaned. "Not again!"

"Just keep moving—and fighting!" Wu yelled.

WHACK! SLAM! WHAM!

The brothers knocked the Grays back one after another, protecting Indi and Mindaro. Indi held her father's elbow, helping him move toward the front of the painting.

Wu glanced behind him and saw a great, pale wall—the front of the painting.

"Almost there!" Wu cried. He thrust his staff into the belly of another Gray, shoving him backward.

Indi and Mindaro reached the wall.

"Father, now!" Indi cried.

Mindaro held up his paintbrush and started drawing the same symbols the brothers had seen on the cave. The pale wall in front of them began to shimmer with magic.

"I am lifting the barrier, so we can communicate with Peri," Mindaro explained. "But if the Chroma tries to escape, I will close it!"

"Peri! We need you!" Indi called out.

The Grays tried to stop Indi and Mindaro.

wHACK!

Garmadon sent a Gray flying with a shove.

SMACK!

Wu kept a Gray at bay with a powerful punch.

"Peri! We need you!" Indi yelled again. "Peri, please!"

Peri's giant face appeared in front of them, her eyes wide with surprise.

"Sister? Father?" she asked. "Oh, it's been so long! I have spent many nights staring at this painting, watching the Chroma howl and roar, with no sign of you. Does this mean the Chroma has been defeated?"

"No, not yet, and we need your help," Indi answered.

wHACK!

"Paint some rainbow colors into this painting, fast!" Garmadon yelled.

"What?" Peri asked.

"There's no time to explain," Indi said. "We have an idea. Father needs some rainbow colors to help these ninja defeat the Chroma."

AAAAAAROOOOOOOOOOOOOOOOOOO!

The Chroma's eerie howl echoed throughout the painting. Wu looked back to see the enormous creature appear on the horizon.

"Peri, hurry!" Wu yelled.

Peri nodded and ducked away. She quickly returned, holding a paintbrush.

BAM! wHAM!

Wu and Garmadon sent two more Grays flying.

"Now, paint!" Indi yelled.

Peri quickly painted a yellow and orange flower on a green stem. As she painted, the flower came to life in front of them.

AAAAAAROOOOOOOOOOOOOOOOOOO!

The Chroma glided toward them across the gray landscape like a coming storm.

"Now, Mindaro!" Wu cried. "Give those colors a boost!"

Mindaro placed both hands, palms up, in front of the flower. He closed his eyes and began to chant under his breath.

Nothing happened.

Mindaro opened his eyes. "My magic is too weak. I can't do it."

wHAM!

Wu tripped a Gray charging toward him. He glanced at his brother. Garmadon was busy fighting Grays as the Chroma raced toward them.

Mindaro, meanwhile, knelt back down. "It is no use! I must close the barrier."

"Father, wait!" Peri said suddenly. "You have the strength to do this. I know you do."

She began to paint, and a small flower appeared in front of Mindaro—a purple flower with five petals.

Why would she paint something so small? Wu wondered, but Mindaro's eyes widened.

"A violet!" he cried.

"Mother always had faith in you," Peri said. "It's not your fault that you couldn't save her. But you can save us now."

Mindaro stood up. A flush of pale pink appeared in his cheeks. He approached the yellow and orange flower and placed his hands on it once more.

AAAAAAAOOOOOOOOOOOOOOOOOOO!

The Chroma was almost upon them now.

"Garmadon, protect Mindaro and Indi!" Wu cried. "I'll try to keep the Chroma at bay."

But his brother was staring up at the Chroma, his eyes flashing with anger.

"You're wrong, Chroma!" Garmadon yelled over the monster's roar. "I'm not—"

He's hearing the Chroma again, Wu realized. *If he freezes, we're all in jeopardy. I've got to get to him, to snap him out of his trance . . .*

Wu was suddenly distracted by Mindaro, whose gray eyes were now violet and sparkling with energy.

He moved his hands in a swirling motion through the flower. The orange, yellow, and green colors began to whirl and twist.

"Peri, more colors!" Indi cried.

More flowers appeared in the painting as Peri painted them—pink, blue, turquoise, red, orange, yellow, green, purple—each flower was more colorful than the next. Mindaro's body began to glow with magical energy as he moved his arms, causing the colors to swirl together into one rainbow ribbon.

It's Spinjitzu time! Wu thought.

"Garmadon, snap out of it!" he yelled. *"Ninjaaaaago!"*

Wu launched into Spinjitzu, slamming into his brother. Garmadon woke from his trance.

"Thanks, brother!" he cried. "I'm so tired of this creature messing with my mind. *Ninjaaaago!"*

Instantly, Garmadon became a spinning tornado, just like Wu.

AAAAAAAOOOOOOOOOOOOOOOOOOOO!

The Chroma descended on them. Its huge mouth opened wide, ready to swallow them all—

Whoosh!

Wu and Garmadon whirled quickly into the magical rainbow of colors created by Peri and Mindaro. They

spun until a swirling rainbow tornado finally formed around them.

Then, together, the two sons of the First Spinjitzu Master hurled the rainbow tornado at the monstrous gray creature in front of them!

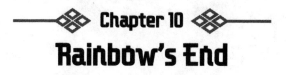

Chapter 10

Rainbow's End

The colors splattered all over the Chroma's body. They swirled through the monster, growing and expanding. Wu and Garmadon stopped spinning and landed, watching the scene in wonder.

The rainbow light spread through the Chroma and outside of it, stretching across the gray landscape and transforming it into a swirl of bright colors. As the Chroma shrieked and wailed, the Grays disappeared underneath the color.

Then . . . *BOOM!* The Chroma exploded into the sky, stretching across it like a giant rainbow.

"We did it!" Garmadon cheered.

"We defeated the Chroma!" Wu said.

Figures then began to fall from the sky. Some of them wore armor, some carried weapons. A lion with wings even fell with them.

They all landed on the ground, looking stunned and confused.

"It's everyone who fought the Chroma!" Indi cried. "They're alive!"

The lion roared.

"Mindaro, do you think you can get us out of here now?" Wu asked.

The magician grinned. "Of course."

He dipped his paintbrush into the center of the nearest flower and then began to paint a portal in the air in front of them. The portal grew bigger and bigger.

"All ready," he said.

Indi jumped through the portal first, and the rest followed eagerly. When Wu and Garmadon jumped through, they found themselves in a room inside the white villa. Indi, Peri, and Mindaro hugged each other, weeping happy tears.

"I thought this day would never come," Peri said.

"We owe our thanks to the ninja," Indi reminded her sister.

Peri turned to the ninja and could not meet their eyes.

"Garmadon, Wu, I am so very sorry," she said. "I should have been honest with you. Forgive me, please. I let my fear rule me."

"It's OK," Garmadon said. "We've all done things we regret."

"That's true," added Wu. "As our father always says, 'Even lessons learned the hard way are lessons learned.'"

"Ahem!" said a woman wearing a red bandana and carrying a sword. "I think ye owe the rest of us an apology, too, lass!"

ROAR! agreed the lion.

"Yes, yes, of course," Peri said. "How can I make it up to you all?"

"By showing us the way out of here!" the man in the horned helmet grunted.

Peri pointed to the mon-dog at her feet, and Balee hopped toward the door.

"This way! This way!" he cried, and the pirate, the explorer, the warrior, and the lion followed him out.

Then they heard a voice from the painting.

"Good job, everyone!"

Jelena, the magical white deer, had jumped into the Chroma painting.

"I had a feeling you ninja would succeed," Jelena said. "This is a very pretty world now, indeed. I shall enjoy exploring it."

"Can't you come out here with the rest of us, Jelena?" Wu asked.

"Yes, Jelena!" Peri added. "I would like to hug you and thank you for all you have done for me. I'm sorry I put you through so much."

Jelena shook her head. "I was created out of paint, and I feel at home in this world," she said. "But don't worry, Peri and Indi. I will always be here, in these paintings, to play with you. Of course, if you want to get Will out of my magical forest, I'd appreciate it."

"Yes, that would be very nice, thanks!" came Will's faint voice from the painting in the other room.

Then the deer trotted off across the rainbow landscape.

Mindaro approached Wu and Garmadon. His beard was still a bushy mess, but his cheeks glowed with health, and his purple eyes sparkled with joy.

"I owe you two a debt," he said. "Thank you for reuniting our family."

"You don't owe us anything," Wu said. "That's what ninja do."

"Unless, of course, Peri wants to give us some veggies for our journey," Garmadon added.

Peri smiled. "I will pack something up for you now. It is the least I can do. For helping us—and for forgiving me."

A short while later Wu and Garmadon said goodbye to Peri, Indi, and Mindaro.

"Balee would be happy to be your guide," Peri offered.

Wu looked down at the little mon-dog and remembered what Jelena had told them: that Balee had been painted by Mindaro. The creature was cute, but they had dealt with enough magical creatures for one adventure.

"That's OK," Wu said. "But thanks for the offer."

Garmadon agreed. "Yeah, getting down is the easy part."

The brothers made their way down the mountain.

Garmadon walked ahead of Wu. "What do you think, Wu? How long before we reach the ocean? I say it's only a couple of days away."

"I say we have no idea what's on the other side of this mountain, so we can't be sure," he said.

"Worrywart Wu," Garmadon teased, and as they walked, Wu studied his brother, thinking.

He heard the Chroma in his head, back there. It all worked out, but there's one thing I'm still confused about. Why did Garmadon hear the Chroma, but not me?

"I hope you're right, Garmadon," Wu said as the brothers continued their journey. "I'll be happy when we find that tea."

"I bet I'll find it before you do," Garmadon said, with a playful grin.

Wu smiled. *This journey has had its ups and downs, but every minute I spend with Garmadon, I feel like our bond grows stronger,* he thought. *Whether we find the tea or not, I'll remember these adventures with my brother forever.*

 **Epilogue**

"Master Wu, what was on the other side of that mountain?" Nya wondered.

"I shall have to tell you that story another time," Wu responded. "I believe we have found what we are looking for."

He put a finger to his lips and pointed to the black and white bird, now perched on top of a display stand holding a necklace made of green stone beads.

"I'll grab it!" Kai hissed.

"Unwise, Kai," Zane said. "Magpies are clever birds. They are well known for stealing shiny objects and hiding them. We must follow it to its stash." Then we can retrieve the necklace.

The bird grabbed the necklace in its beak and flew off. The heavy necklace weighed it down, and it couldn't outfly the ninja. They followed it to a gallery of paintings, where it dropped to the floor.

The bird stuffed the necklace into a hole at the bottom of the wall.

"Now can I grab it?" Kai asked.

"If you can," Zane replied.

Kai dove for the bird with his arms outstretched. The bird flew away. Lloyd jumped up and opened a small window near the top of the ceiling, and the bird flew outside. Lloyd quickly slammed it shut and dropped down.

Nya, meanwhile, had investigated the bird's stash.

"It's stuffed with jewelry," she reported. "You were right, Zane. We've found our thief."

Kai shrugged his shoulders. "I guess this was pretty routine after all."

"Cheer up, Kai," Jay said. "We solved the case, and at least we heard a good story."

"Speaking of the story," Cole said. "Look at this painting!"

He pointed to the wall, where a large painting hung. It showed a landscape with rolling hills in the

background. Colorful flowers dotted the grass. A large rainbow stretched across a bright blue sky, adding a spark of joy to the peaceful scene.

"Master Wu, that's like the painting in your story!" Nya cried. Excited, she ran toward it. "It's signed by Mindaro. This is it!"

Master Wu frowned. "Interesting. I am not sure how it ended up here in the museum."

"We should get this jewelry to the museum director," Lloyd said. "Maybe we can ask there."

"Certainly," Master Wu replied, and they picked up the jewelry and left the room. Master Wu stopped, cast one worried glance behind him, and then joined the ninja. "I'm sure there is nothing to worry about," he muttered.

Behind him, a small gray cloud appeared in the painting's blue sky.

 Glossary

Balee

This unusual creature— who is half-monkey, half-dog— finds Wu and Garmadon in the fog of the mountain vegetation and leads them to Peri's house. Balee also has the ability to speak, but Wu isn't sure if the mon-dog just repeats what he hears or has thoughts of his own.

The Chroma

The Chroma is a monster trapped inside a painting. Many warriors have tried to punch or kick it into submission, only to be consumed by it.

Cole

Cole is a member of Master Wu's ninja team. As the Earth Ninja, he wields the elemental power of Earth and supports his friends with his confidence and great physical strength.

First Spinjitzu Master

This is the creator of Spinjitzu and the entire Ninjago world. He was also the father of Garmadon and Wu, whom he trained in the art of Spinjitzu to protect the world he had created.

Garmadon

A son of the First Spinjitzu Master, Garmadon grew up learning the ways of Spinjitzu with his brother, Wu. Bitten by a vile snake, Garmadon gradually filled with evil to become Lord Garmadon, the greatest villain in the world of Ninjago.

Grays

These creepy, human-like, gray figures are the Chroma's first line of defense.

Indi

She is Peri's younger sister, who tried to save their father. Now she is helping Wu and Garmadon to find and confront the Chroma.

Jay

The Lightning Ninja is quick-witted, talks fast, and often acts before he thinks. Jay also loves pranks and jokes. Without Jay's sense of humor, the ninja team would be in a much worse mood.

Jelena

This large, white deer with sparkling eyes and crystal antlers guides the ninja to Indi and Mindaro.

Kai

This is Nya's older brother, the Fire Ninja. With his fierce temper, bravery, and strong sense of justice, Kai will stop at nothing if he has put his mind to it.

Lloyd

The leader of the ninja team is the son of Garmadon and Misako. Lloyd once sought to follow in his father's evil footsteps, but with the help of the ninja, he fulfilled his destiny to become the Green Ninja.

Mindaro

Peri and Indi's father is an amazingly talented magician with a desire to preserve the natural beauty of the world of Ninjago. One of Mindaro's unique powers is creating realistic paintings that come to life.

Nya

Kai's younger sister is the Water Ninja. She's a skilled warrior, inventor, and tech wiz. She's often the team's voice of reason and a steadfast support to her friends.

Peri

She is a mysterious young woman who invites Wu and Garmadon to stay. Peri is willing to share her food, her home, and her paintings, but is reluctant to tell the ninja where the rest of her family is.

Spinjitzu

This is an ancient technique based on balance and rotation in which one taps their elemental energy while turning quickly. Developed by the father of Garmadon and Wu, Spinjitzu is not only a martial art, but also a way of living. Mastering it is a lifelong journey.

Time Twins

The Masters of Time, Krux and Acronix, also known as the Time Twins, once stood side by side with

Master Wu and other Elemental Masters. But their hunger for power led to a conflict that almost caused the destruction of Ninjago world. For young Wu and Garmadon, it is still something to happen in the future.

Will

A traveling barber with a curly mustache, Will describes himself as a worrier.

Wu

Wu is the other son of the First Spinjitzu Master, and little brother to Garmadon. After many years of mastering the art of Spinjitzu and the ways of the ninja, Wu shares his knowledge with his students—Lloyd, Kai, Cole, Jay, Zane, and Nya—to train them as ninja protectors of the world of Ninjago.

Zane

Brave and caring Zane is the Titanium Ninja, wielding the elemental power of ice. He is a Nindroid (ninja robot), created to protect those who cannot protect themselves.